Created and Written by
Scott Christian Sava

Art by
Andres Silva Blanco

Color Assist by
Joseph Bergin III

www.IDWpublishing.com

ISBN: 978-1-60010-315-5

12 11 10 09   1 2 3 4

Production by Robbie Robbins • Edited by Justin Eisinger

Operations: Ted Adams, Chief Executive Officer • Greg Goldstein, Chief Operating Officer • Matthew Ruzicka, CPA, Chief Financial Officer • Alan Payne, VP of Sales • Lorelei Bunjes, Dir. of Digital Services • Marci Hubbard, Executive Assistant • Alonzo Simon, Shipping Manager • **Editorial:** Chris Ryall, Publisher/Editor-in-Chief • Scott Dunbier, Editor, Special Projects • Andy Schmidt, Senior Editor • Justin Eisinger, Editor • Kris Oprisko, Editor/Foreign Lic. • Denton J. Tipton, Editor • Tom Waltz, Editor • Mariah Huehner, Associate Editor • **Design:** Robbie Robbins, EVP/Sr. Graphic Artist • Ben Templesmith, Artist/Designer • Neil Uyetake, Art Director • Chris Mowry, Graphic Artist • Amauri Osorio, Graphic Artist

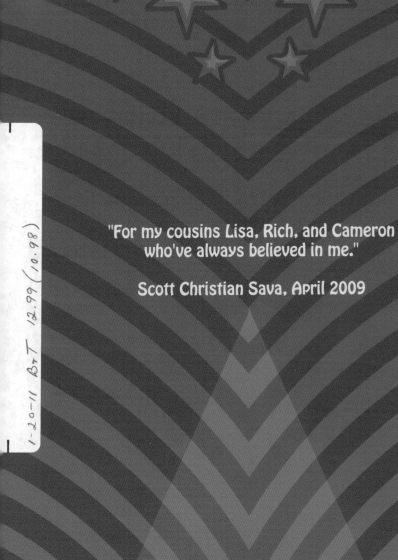

"For my cousins Lisa, Rich, and Cameron
who've always believed in me."

Scott Christian Sava, April 2009

RISE, MY CHILDREN. RISE AND MEET YOUR *MASTER*.

ARISE, MIGHTY *TRICERATOPS*!

YOU ARE A MASTER OF DEFENSE. *NIGH IMPERVIOUS TO HARM*. YOU SHALL BE THE *TACTICIAN* OF THE GROUP.

AND I SHALL CALL YOU....

LIZZY.

AWAKEN, LORD OF THE SKIES! AWAKEN MAGNIFICENT *PTERODACTYL!*

YOU ARE A MASTER OF *STEALTH.* YOU ARE *THE EYES OF THE TEAM* AND SHALL BE IN CHARGE OF RECONNAISSANCE.

AND I SHALL NAME YOU...

DEE DEE!

RISE, KING OF THE DINOSAURS. RISE *TYRANNOSAURUS REX!*

YOU ARE *VICIOUS.* YOU ARE *TERROR INCARNATE!* YOU KNOW *NO FEAR!* YOU ARE THE *PERFECT SOLDIER!*

I SHALL NAME YOU...

CHARLIE.

UP! UP MY GREATEST....

ARISE GREAT BEAST OF....

FALLBROOK MIDDLE SCHOOL

AND IT IS MY THEORY THAT IF *DINOSAURS* WALKED THE EARTH TODAY...THEY WOULD BE ABLE TO COMMUNICATE WITH US THROUGH LANGUAGE.

I KNOW THEIR *BRAINS* IN RELATION TO THEIR SIZE IS MINISCULE. BUT THEY'RE STILL LIKE *10 TIMES THE SIZE OF OUR BRAINS.* THAT HAS TO COUNT FOR *SOMETHING.*

CLAP CLAP CLAP CLAP

THAT'S A WONDERFUL BIT OF...UH...*SCIENCE FICTION* THERE CAMERON. BUT WELL SAID.

12

HEY. YOU *LEARNED* SOMETHING.

THANKS. I WASN'T A BIG FAN OF DINOSAURS *BEFORE* THIS REPORT...BUT I HAVE TO ADMIT...THEY'RE PRETTY *INCREDIBLE.*

I GUESS I'M DOING *SOMETHING* RIGHT AS A TEACHER.

HA HA HA HA HA HA HA

BBRRRRIIIIINNNGGGGGGGG

OK CLASS. PLEASE DON'T FORGET WE HAVE A FIELD TRIP TO *PINKERTON PARK* TOMORROW.

BRING YOUR PERMISSION SLIPS!

WHAT DO YOU *MEAN* YOU WON'T DO MY BIDDING?

YOU **HAVE** TO OBEY ME!

I CREATED YOU!

AND WE APPRECIATE THAT *PROFESSOR POPPYCOCK*.

ALL OF US REALLY DO.

BUT YOU CREATED US WITH *SUPERIOR INTELLECT*.

WE CAN'T IN GOOD CONSCIENCE DO THE EVIL THAT YOU WANT FROM US.

WE DON'T WANT TO HURT ANYONE.

SO WHILE WE APPRECIATE YOU *CREATING US*...WE FEEL WE MUST LEAVE NOW, PROFESSOR POPPYCOCK.

NO NO NO!

I COMMAND YOU! STOP RIGHT NOW.

HALT!

CEASE!

DESIST!

MIGHT I SUGGEST YOU *RE-THINK* YOUR PROFESSION *PROFESSOR POPPYCOCK.*

TRY AND USE YOUR ABILITIES FOR GOOD INSTEAD OF EVIL.

MAYBE SEEK SOME *PROFESSIONAL* HELP.

THIRTY MILLION DOLLARS AND FIFTEEN YEARS OF MY LIFE....

...JUST WALKED OUT THAT DOOR.

WHAT AM I GOING TO TELL **MY INVESTORS?!**

PINKERTON PARK

...AND THROUGH CAREFUL DIGGING AND A LOT OF PATIENCE...

...WE WERE ABLE TO UNCOVER BONES OF A WONDERFUL CREATURE CALLED THE *DIPLODOCUS.*

I BELIEVE THIS WAS HIS *FUNNY BONE.*

HA HA HA HA HA HA HA HA HA HA HA HA HA HA HA HA HA

DOCTOR KELAITA, WHAT ELSE CAN YOU TELL US OF THE MAGNITUDE OF YOUR DISCOVERY?

WELL...THE DIPLODOCUS...AND *OTHER* DINOSAURS THAT WE'VE FOUND HERE AREN'T *COMMON* IN THIS AREA.

THIS *COULD* INDICATE SOME SORT OF *MIGRATION*.

OR POSSIBLY TELL US MORE ABOUT THE *LAND MASSES* OF MILLIONS OF YEARS AGO.

EITHER WAY, IT ALLOWS US TO BE *CLOSER* TO THESE NOW EXTINCT CREATURES AND HELPS US TO KNOW MORE *ABOUT* THEM.

HEY *GUYS*. MS. LISA ASKED ME TO SNAP SOME PICTURES FOR THE SCHOOL PAPER.

WANNA COME?

NAH. I'M JUST GONNA SIT HERE UNTIL THIS WINDBAG IS DONE TALKING.

ME TOO. IT'S *TOO HOT* TO GO ANYWHERE.

FINE. SUIT YOURSELVES.

I'LL BE BACK.

YOU *LOST* THEM???

HOW DO YOU LOSE *DINOSAURS???*

BUT BUT BUT... *I HAD THEM....HERE...*

...AND AND AND...THEY SAID THEY DON'T WANT TO DO *EVIL...*

THEN...THEN THEY TOLD ME TO GO *SEE A SHRINK* AND I...

DO YOU THINK I'M CRAZY? DO I NEED PROFESSIONAL HELP?

THE *BROTHERHOOD OF UNIVERSAL REVOLUTION FOR POLITICAL SUBTERFUGE.* THAT'S TOO LONG. YOU SHOULD JUST SHORTEN IT TO *B.U.R.P.S.*

MAYBE. MAYBE YOU'RE NOT GETTING THE *BIG PICTURE* HERE PROFESSOR POPPYCOCK.

YOU SEE. WE AT THE **BROTHERHOOD OF UNIVERSAL REVOLUTION FOR POLITICAL SUBTERFUGE** HAVE AN...

B.U.R.P.S.

FINE! *B.U.R.P.S.* OK?

WE AT....

SIGH...

...*B.U.R.P.S.* HAVE AN AGENDA. WE ARE PLANNING ON OVERTAKING THE GOVERNMENT AND *KIDNAPPING THE PRESIDENT* WHEN HE VISITS THE CITY.

VERY AMBITIOUS OF YOU.

YES. WE THINK SO AS WELL.

BUT YOU SEE? WE REALLY THINK WE CAN DO SOMETHING *TRULY EVIL* WITH B.U.R.P.S.

BUT WE CAN'T KIDNAP THE PRESIDENT AND OVERTHROW THE GOVERNMENT *WITHOUT....*

DINOSAURS?

EXACTLY!

NOW. WE HAVE THREE WEEKS UNTIL THE PRESIDENT ARRIVES IN THE CITY.

YOU *WILL* HAVE DINOSAURS FOR US.

BUT I DON'T...

YOU *WILL* GIVE US DINOSAURS!

CLICK

CLICK

WHAT THE *HECK?*

AAAAH! *PLEASE DON'T EAT ME!!!!*

MY DINOSAURS WERE *PERFECT.* THEY WERE *WORKS OF ART.*

SO WHERE DID I GO WRONG?

HOW DID I *MISCALCULATE?*

WAIT! I BELIEVE I KNOW *WHAT MUST BE DONE.*

YES...THESE OLD DESIGNS MAY HAVE THE **ANSWERS I SEEK.**

MY ONLY FLAW IN CREATING THOSE **BLASTED DINOSAURS** WAS GIVING THEM *FREE WILL.*

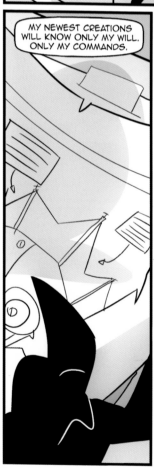

MY NEWEST CREATIONS WILL KNOW ONLY MY WILL. ONLY MY COMMANDS.

THEY WILL DO *EVERYTHING I TELL THEM TO DO!*

MUWAHAHAHAA!!!

...AND THAT'S HOW WE GOT HERE.

REALLY?

REALLY.

SO LET ME GET THIS STRAIGHT.

YOU CAME FROM OLD *POPPYCOCK MANOR.*

PROFESSOR POINDEXTER P. POPPYCOCK **CREATED YOU FROM REAL DINOSAUR DNA?**

TO WORK FOR AN EVIL COMPANY CALLED **B.U.R.P.S.**

THAT'S WHAT PROFESSOR POPPYCOCK CALLED THEM.

AND THEY WANTED YOU TO *TAKE OVER* THE GOVERNMENT.

YEAH. SO WE LEFT.

AND HERE YOU ARE?

HERE WE ARE.

WOW.

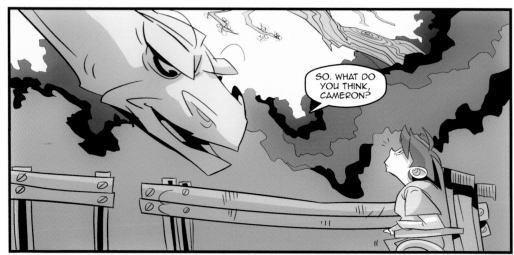

SO. WHAT DO YOU THINK, CAMERON?

YOU'RE SUPPOSED TO BE *EXTINCT!*

I HAVE NO IDEA WHAT TO DO!

I'M ONLY *11 YEARS OLD!*

WELL, ARE THERE ANY *ADULTS* WHO COULD HELP US?

MY TEACHER MAYBE. BUT SHE'D PROBABLY *FAINT* IF SHE SAW YOU.

THE *PRINCIPAL* IS HERE.

BUT HE'D SOMEHOW FIND A WAY TO MAKE THIS *MY* FAULT AND GIVE ME *DETENTION*.

WAIT. DOCTOR KELAITA!

WHO?

HE'S THE ARCHEOLOGIST WHO'S IN CHARGE OF THIS PLACE. HE KNOWS *EVERYTHING ABOUT DINOSAURS.*

AND YOU THINK HE CAN HELP US?

HE HAS TO. WAIT HERE.

I UH...
I CAN'T TELL YOU.

YOU CAN'T?
WHY?

PLEASE
DOCTOR KELAITA.
*JUST FOLLOW
ME!*

CAMERON! WHAT ARE YOU DOING
INTERRUPTING DOCTOR KELAITA'S
LECTURE LIKE THIS?

THIS ISN'T HOW
WE BEHAVE ON
FIELD TRIPS!

I THINK IT'S WONDERFUL THAT YOUNG...

...UM...

CAMERON.

CAMERON HERE FINDS ARCHEOLOGY SO EXCITING.

NOW IF YOU'LL EXCUSE US.

I BELIEVE YOUNG CAMERON HERE IS ABOUT TO ASTOUND ME WITH HIS NEW DISCOVERY.

AAAAAAAHHHHHHH!!!!

DOCTOR KELAITA, WAIT!

DINOSAURS!

THEY'RE REAL!

THEY'RE GOING TO EAT ME!

THEY'RE **NOT** GOING TO EAT YOU, DOCTOR KELAITA.

HUFF PUFF HUFF PUFF. GULP.

THEY. THEY'RE NOT?

WELL... ALL OF US EXCEPT CHARLIE OVER THERE.

NO. THEY'RE PLANT EATERS.

BUT I'M COOL. I HAD A FEW SHEEP FOR LUNCH EARLIER AT THE FARM NEARBY.

AAAH!

THEY CAN TALK???

THEY'VE BEEN GONE FOR QUITE SOME TIME NOW. SHOULD I BE GETTING *WORRIED?*

NO. DOCTOR KELAITA IS PROBABLY HUMORING YOUR STUDENT. TELLING HIM A *ROCK* HE FOUND IS A *VELOCIRAPTOR* SKULL OR SOMETHING.

HE HE, HE HE HE HE HE HE

KIDS. THEY HAVE *SUCH* ACTIVE IMAGINATIONS.

THANK YOU ALL FOR YOUR PATIENCE.

50

YOUNG CAMERON HERE HAS MADE AN **ASTOUNDING** DISCOVERY.

WHAT IS IT? MORE BONES?

FOOTPRINTS?

FOSSILIZED EGGS?

NO NO NO, NOTHING SO TRIVIAL.

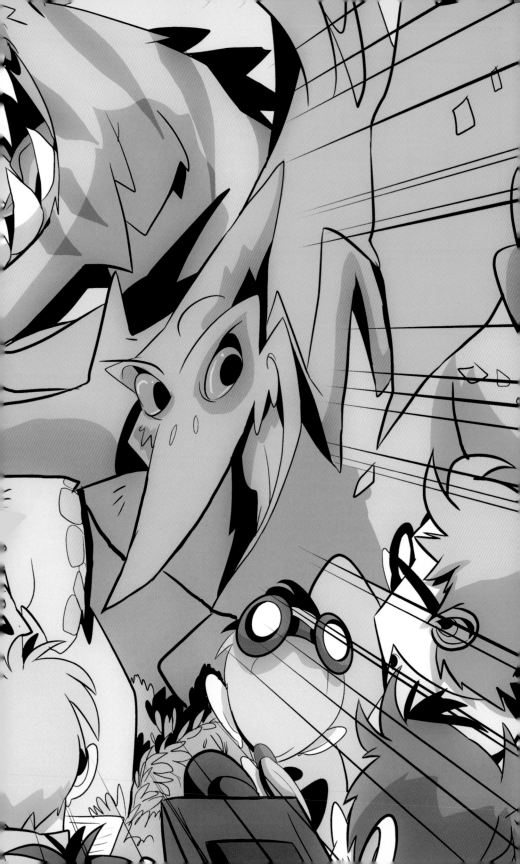

...NEWS YESTERDAY. A YOUNG BOY HAS FOUND ACTUAL *LIVING DINOSAURS* ON A *SCHOOL FIELD TRIP.*

ARCHEOLOGIST DOCTOR RICHARD KELAITA HAS ASSURED THE AUTHORITIES THAT THEY ARE INDEED FRIENDLY.

IT SEEMS THAT THE DINOSAURS NAMED LIZZY, DEE DEE, CHARLIE, AND VINNIE ARE FAST BECOMING *CELEBRITIES.*

THE DINOSAURS HAVE BEEN MOVED TO A SECURED GOVERNMENT FACILITY TO ENSURE THEIR SAFETY.

BAH!

CRASH

CELEBRITIES? MY DINOSAURS?

IF ANYONE SHOULD BE FAMOUS...IT SHOULD BE ME!

AFTER ALL... I'M THE *GENIUS* WHO *CREATED* THEM.

I TRUST YOU'RE COMFORTABLE HERE.

WE'VE HAD THE SCIENTISTS BRING IN VEGETATION FROM ALL AROUND THE WORLD IN HOPES OF MAKING YOUR STAY AS PLEASING AS POSSIBLE.

THIS IS GREAT. THESE PLANTS ARE WONDERFUL. THANKS.

61

THANKS, GENERAL CLAYTON, FOR LETTING ME SEE THEM AGAIN.

YOU'RE WELCOME *ANY* TIME HERE, SON.

YOUR FRIENDS HAVE TOLD US ALL ABOUT *PROFESSOR POPPYCOCK* AND THE *BROTHERHOOD OF UNIVERSAL REVOLUTION FOR POLITICAL SUBTERFUGE'S* PLAN TO OVERTHROW THE GOVERNMENT.

AND WE'RE PLEASED TO SAY THEY'VE OFFERED THEIR ASSISTANCE IN PRESERVING THE PEACE.

WE'LL USE THIS FACILITY AS OUR BASE OF OPERATION.

FOR NOW, THEY'LL CALL THIS...HOME.

GENERAL, WOULD IT BE ALRIGHT IF CAMERON COMES BY AFTER SCHOOL TO VISIT EVERY ONCE AND A WHILE?

AS LONG AS IT'S OK WITH HIS PARENTS.

WE'LL GET YOU A CLEARANCE PASS, SON.

YOU CAN COME BY AND VISIT YOUR FRIENDS EVERY DAY.

WOW! THANKS!

RING TOSS WITH LIZZY!

WATCHING THEIR FAVORITE T.V. PROGRAM... THE FANNIE WINKLEHAM SHOW!

BEST FRIENDS FOR LIFE!

HEY GUYS.

WHAT'S GOING ON?

WELL CAMERON. GENERAL CLAYTON BROUGHT YOU A *SURPRISE*.

SURPRISE? FOR WHAT?

OUR BOYS OVER AT THE TECH DEPARTMENT WERE *TINKERING* AROUND WITH SOME GADGETS ...AND...

ZOOOM

HA HA.
LOOK AT THAT KID GO.
HE'S A NATURAL.

I...UH.
I HAVE A
REQUEST FOR YOU,
GENERAL CLAYTON.

WHAT IS IT,
DOCTOR?

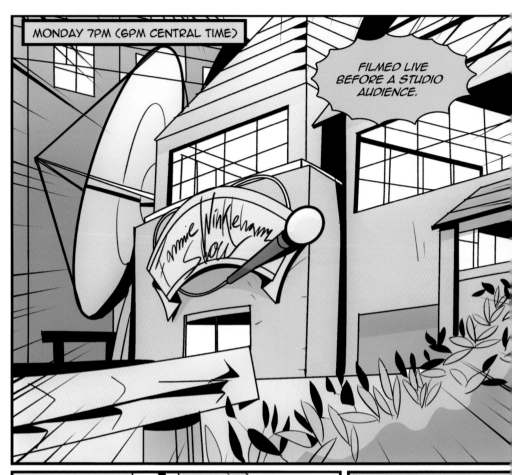

FILMED LIVE BEFORE A STUDIO AUDIENCE.

THIS IS SO EXCITING!

I'M STILL AGAINST THIS.

WoOOOOO

WOW. THEY LOVE US.

WELL AT LEAST THEY'RE NOT SCREAMING AND RUNNING AWAY.

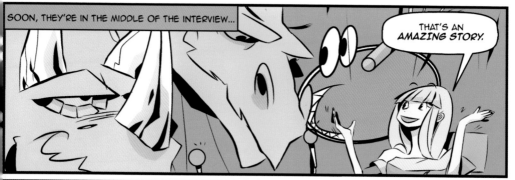

THAT'S AN *AMAZING STORY.*

ISN'T THAT AN *AMAZING STORY?*

WOOOOOO!

SO... WHERE IS THIS YOUNG BOY *CAMERON?* IS HE HERE TONIGHT WITH YOU?

YEAH SURE. HE'S RIGHT THERE BACKSTAGE.

COME ON EVERYONE. LET'S WELCOME *CAMERON.*

CLAP CLAP CLAP

THE BRAVE YOUNG BOY WHO DISCOVERED THE DINOSAURS.

GO ON, CAMERON. THE WORLD IS WAITING TO MEET YOU.

CLAP CLAP CLAP

WHAT'S GOING ON? WHERE DID THEY GO?

I THINK THEY'RE UP ON THE ROOF.

ALRIGHT, PROFESSOR POPPYCOCK. WE KNOW YOU'RE UP THERE WITH THE BOY AND FANNIE WINKLEHAM!

YOU'RE COMPLETELY SURROUNDED AND OUTGUNNED.

WE DEMAND THAT YOU RELEASE YOUR PRISONERS AND SURRENDER TO US IMMEDIATELY.

THIS IS THE U.S. ARMY.

RELEASE YOUR PRISONERS, DEACTIVATE YOUR ROBOTIC DINOSAUR, AND SURRENDER IMMEDIATELY.

PTERANODON. PLEASE REMOVE THOSE ANNOYING THINGS.

THEY'RE MESSING UP MY HAIRS.

CRASH

THOSE HELICOPTERS ARE NO MATCH FOR THAT ROBOTIC PTERANODON.

THIS IS YOUR *LAST WARNING*, PROFESSOR POPPYCOCK.

RELEASE THE PRISONERS NOW AND WE CA–

SPLAT

SPLISH

YOU WANT TO PLAY ROUGH, PROFESSOR?

ODIN'S BEARD TO BARREL OF MONKEYS. WE ARE GO FOR **OPERATION BOOM BOOM.**

I REPEAT. WE ARE GO FOR **OPERATION BOOM BOOM!**

RUMBLE
RUMBLE

RUMBLE
RUMBLE
RUMBLE

WHAT'S THAT?

AN EARTHQUAKE?

NO. THAT'S NOT AN EARTHQUAKE...

THAT'S OPERATION BOOM BOOM!

HISSSSSSS!

HISSSSSSS!

HISSSSSSS!

FANNIE WINKLEHAM, I'M SHOCKED.

WERE YOU GOING TO *BASH* ME ON THE HEAD WITH THAT PIPE?

IS THAT ANY WAY TO TREAT A MEMBER OF YOUR *FAN CLUB?*

110

BOOP!

BUZZ
BUZZ
BUZZ

POPPYCOCK!
YOU IMBECILE!
WHAT ARE
YOU DOING??

I....I...I...

THESE DINOSAURS WERE TO BE USED TO **CAPTURE THE PRESIDENT!**

NOT FOR YOU TO PLAY WITH.

WE'RE TAKING OVER FROM HERE ON OUT.

BOOP

ZZRT

THIS IS HOPELESS.

THEY'RE TEARING THROUGH YOUR MEN LIKE THEY WERE TOYS.

WE'VE GOT TO HELP OUT.

HELP?

HOW? YOU'RE NO MATCH FOR THOSE MONSTROSITIES??

GENERAL, PLEASE REMEMBER, WE WERE DESIGNED FOR ACTION.

WE MAY NOT BE AS STRONG AS THEY ARE.

BUT WE CAN HELP.

GIVE MY MEN A FEW MORE MOMENTS. SEE IF THEY CAN TURN THE TIDE.

GENERAL!

CAMERON! YOU'RE ALRIGHT!

YES. THANKS TO FANNIE.

WHAT?

GENERAL. THOSE ROBOTS AREN'T BEING CONTROLLED BY THE PROFESSOR ANYMORE.

IF NOT THE PROFESSOR, THEN WHO?

B.U.R.P.S.

AND THEY'RE AFTER THE PRESIDENT.

GREAT GOOGLEY MOOGLEY!

MY FRIENDS, I'M AFRAID I'M GOING TO HAVE TO TAKE YOU UP ON YOUR OFFER TO HELP.

THANK YOU, GENERAL.

SERGEANT! LET'S GET THESE DINOSAURS HOOKED UP WITH SOME EQUIPMENT AND SEND THEM OUT THERE *ASAP!*

YES SIR!

THIS WAY.

...AND EVERY WHERE THAT MARY WENT, THE LAMB WAS SURE TO GO...

GENERAL. WE'RE HANDLING THESE OTHER DINOSAURS OK.

BUT THE VELOCIRAPTORS HAVE BROKEN OFF FROM THE FIGHT AND ARE HEADING AWAY FROM US.

AWAY FROM YOU?

WHERE COULD THE VELOCIRAPTORS BE HEADED?

GET HIM OUT OF HERE!

THEY'RE GOING AFTER THE PRESIDENT, SILLY.

BUT YOU CAN'T STOP THEM! NO ONE CAN NOW!

I SAID GET HIM OUT!

UNLESS THEY HAVE THIS.

HOLD ON, LET HIM SPEAK.

THAT'LL STOP THEM?

IT'S A NEURAL INHIBITOR. I MADE IT TO CANCEL OUT THEIR *PNEUMONIC BRAINS* IN CASE THEY MALFUNCTIONED.

JUST HOLD IT 3 FEET FROM *THEIR BRAIN* AND IT DISENGAGES THEIR SYNAPTICS.

MAAAYBBBEEEE.

THANKS!

BONK

HEY! NO FAIR!

OW!

135

JUST AS WELL. HE'LL NEVER BE ABLE TO CATCH THOSE VELOCIRAPTORS.

HOW FAST CAN THAT BOY'S HOVER CHAIR GO?

THEY CAN RUN AT SPEEDS OF OVER *120 MILES AN HOUR.*

HAHAHAHAHA

SERGEANT! GET ME THE MANUAL ON THAT HOVER CHAIR OF HIS. NOW!

SMASH

YEAH, GENERAL. I CAN.

LOOK, SON. THOSE VELOCIRAPTORS CAN RUN VERY... *VERY FAST.*

I NEED YOU TO ACTIVATE A CONTROL ON YOUR HOVER CHAIR FOR ME.

OKAY....

HISSSSSSSS!

HISSSSSSSS!

PROTECT THE PRESIDENT.

READY.

AIM.

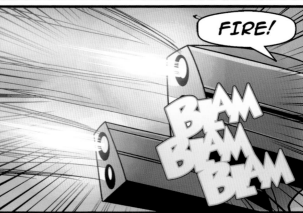

FIRE!

BLAM
BLAM
BLAM

THAT BOY IS DEACTIVATING THOSE ROBOTS, SIR.

AMAZING.

WHAT A BRAVE YOUNG BOY!

WE SHOULD GIVE HIM A MEDAL OR SOMETHING.

ARR-AARK?!

MUNCH

YU URUN UNNA AKE AWW UH HUN AWAY HUNUS. UR YU?

CLANG!

YEAH.
WE'RE A TEAM.
RIGHT?

SLAM

A TEAM...YES...

C:/SCREEE...
.:/BZZT....EEE?

WE'RE A GOOD TEAM.

BUT MOSTLY...

SCREE....ZZT....EEEE....KKKK

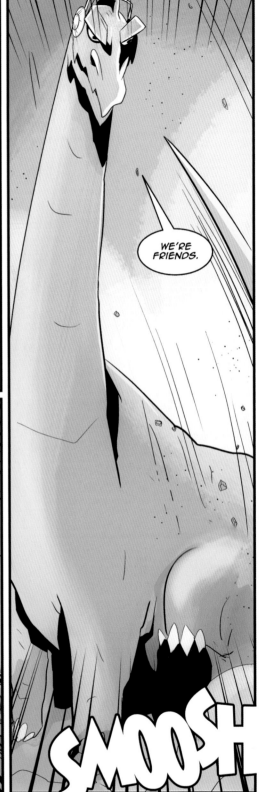

WE'RE FRIENDS.

SMOOSH

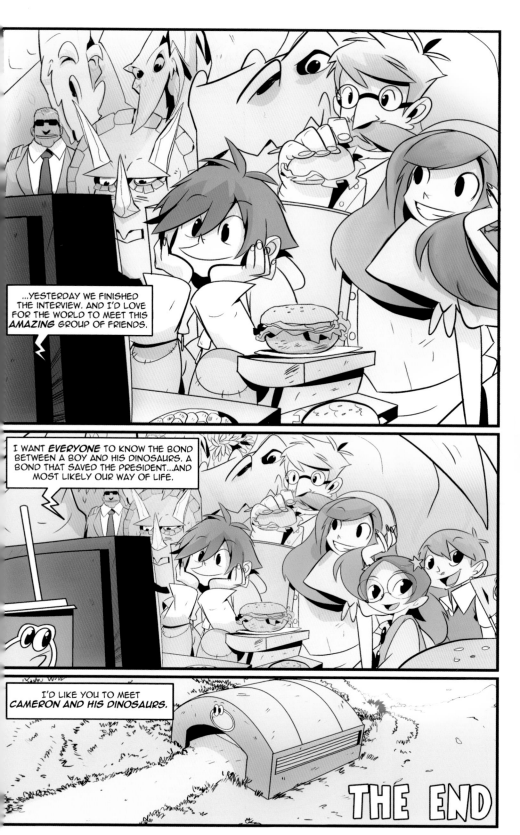

...YESTERDAY WE FINISHED THE INTERVIEW. AND I'D LOVE FOR THE WORLD TO MEET THIS *AMAZING* GROUP OF FRIENDS.

I WANT *EVERYONE* TO KNOW THE BOND BETWEEN A BOY AND HIS DINOSAURS. A BOND THAT SAVED THE PRESIDENT...AND MOST LIKELY OUR WAY OF LIFE.

I'D LIKE YOU TO MEET *CAMERON AND HIS DINOSAURS.*

THE END